Copyright © 1989 by Marian Goldner
Published by Banmar, Inc.
Distributed by Seven Hills Book Distributors
49 Central Avenue, Cincinnati, Ohio

Library of Congress Cataloging-in-Publication Data

Grandma, Marian.
  Mrs. Pam Polar Bear.

  Summary: Mrs. Pam Polar Bear gives birth to her
cubs in a cave in the snow and later risks her life
to defend them from their worst enemy, man.
  [1. Polar bear—Fiction. 2. Bears—Fiction.
3. Stories in rhyme] I. Sullo, Lorraine T., ill.
II. Title.
PZ8.3.G7415Mr 1989   [E]   89-6496
ISBN 0-9614989-9-4

Printed in Hungary

MRS. PAM POLAR BEAR

by Grandma Marian

Illustrated by Lorraine T. Sullo

for Andrea, Mark, Sharon, Jordan & Olivia

BANMAR INC.

New York, New York
1989

If you are a person who likes kind, loving care,
Then you ought to know Mrs. Pam Polar Bear.

She looks kind of scary when seen at the zoo,
But I think you'll love her when my story is through.

Pam looks like most bears, except that she's white,
So in the great snow fields she can be out of sight.

Her home is the Arctic on a polar ice floe.
It is bitter cold there, and icy winds blow.

But she doesn't mind for her fur keeps her warm.
They say she's been seen in the worst kind of storm!

Small creatures love Pam. She protects them, you see.
So when she is around, they romp happily.

Just for fun, she might sneak
Under water to scare
Eider or scoter ducks
Who also live there.

BOO!

A sea gull would perch on Pam's head with a fish,
And Pam would say, "Thanks for the nice tasty dish!"

In spring, when she's tired of all kinds of fishes,
She finds leaves and berries are simply delicious.

But even in snow storms and things of that kind,
She keeps searching for food for it's quite hard to find.

Well, winter was coming, so before it began,
Pam started digging, for she had a plan.

She dug a deep tunnel in the tightly packed snow
And made it slant down toward the hard ice below.

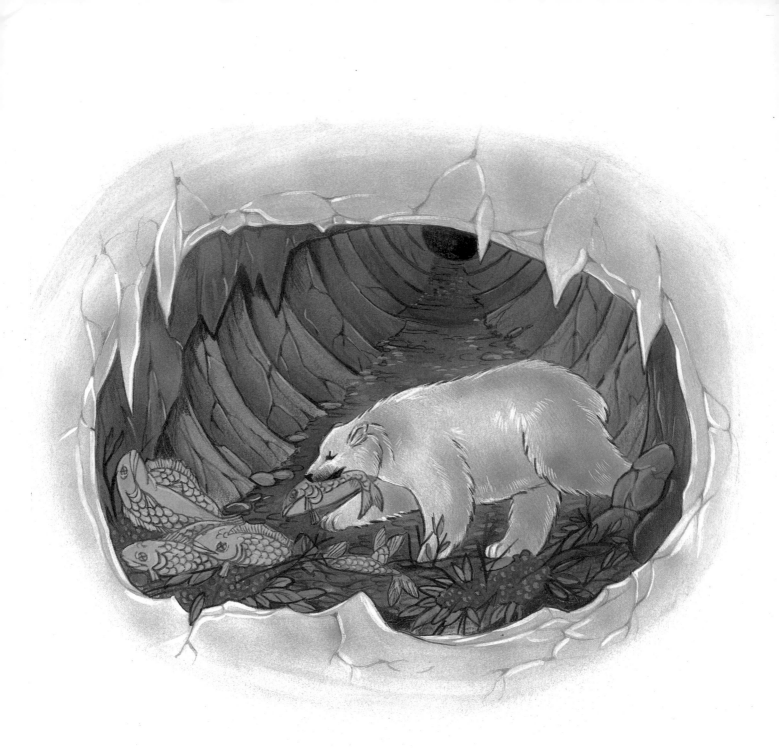

Then she dug a nice cave to be used as a den,
Went out for some food and came back again.

Inside that shelter or chamber or lair,
It was pleasant and cozy, at least for a bear.

By then Pam was tired, so she rested a while.
And then something happened that would just make you smile.

In case you can't guess, she gave birth to twin bears,
Warm and safe by their mama with no worries or cares.

Their eyes weren't open. They were helpless and frail,
Without any fur from their head to their tail.

You should have seen Pam, how she cared for each cubby.
They drank her warm milk, grew white fur and got chubby.

She washed them and loved them and sang a bear song
Until April or May when spring came along.

Then she took the cubs out for fresh air and a snack.
They liked it so well that they never went back!

Outside they found
Other cubs by the dozens
Who looked so alike
That they must have been cousins.

As they romped in the snow,
I would watch with delight
For they looked like big snowballs
All furry and white.

They played tag as they scooted
Through the deep drifts of snow.
Then they splashed in the ocean
And swam to and fro.

Pam took them for rides
On her back which they loved,
But instead of behaving,
They tickled and shoved.

Pam didn't mind though, for she was their mother,
And moms don't tease children like a sister or brother.

Instead, she'd protect them from the freezing wind's might,
And tow them through ice floes while they held on tight.

It was Pam who went out to find them good food,
She would guard while they ate and let no one intrude.

One day, when the bear cubs were playing around,
They heard a strange beast make a frightening sound.

Though the waters were calm and no danger in sight,
Pam felt something evil in the arctic twilight.

Now Pam always cautioned
Her children before,
"If danger appears,
Swim right back to shore!"

But they kept on swimming
Way out to the sea,
Just having fun,
Feeling safe, feeling free.

Within half a minute a stranger appeared—
A man with a gun! Just what Pam always feared!

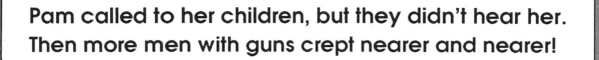

Pam called to her children, but they didn't hear her.
Then more men with guns crept nearer and nearer!

Pam dived in the water. She swam smooth and fast,
When the sound of a rifle made an echoing blast.

The water turned red
As Pam swam along.
Her pace seemed to falter,
For something was wrong.

She was hit in the paw.
But Pam kept swimming on.
She would protect her cubs
Until danger was gone.

When she reached both the cubs,
they were frightened and cried,
"Mama, oh Mama, where can we hide?"

Pam dragged her babies
To the farthest ice floe,
Way out in the ocean
Where those men couldn't go.

When the children were safe cuddled up by her side,
Pam licked her wound 'til it was all clean and dried.

Soon they all fell asleep. When they awoke it all seemed
Like it never had happened, like something they dreamed.

But they learned to mind mother, it's just being smart.
She might scold, but she loves them with all of her heart.

THE END